CW00842022

THE GIRL WHO WALKED
TO THE
MOON

WRITTEN AND ILLUSTRATED BY TESSA YATES

PUBLISHED BY THE HAPPY BOOK COMPANY

FIRST EDITION

WWW.THEHAPPYBOOKCOMPANY.COM

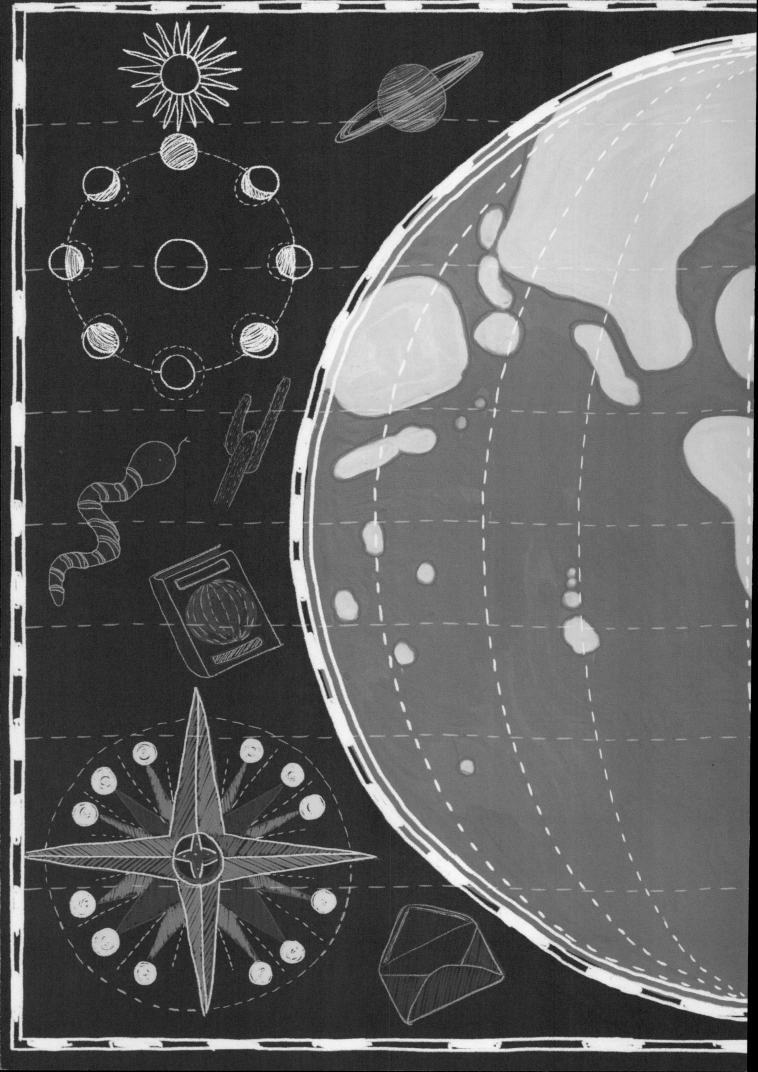

Say "hello" to Tessa, who dreams one day soon
to be the first woman to land on the moon.

"I'll fly in a rocket past birds, trees and kites,
past jet-planes and storm-clouds
and huge satellites."

"I'll slingshot around it
then land with a bump.
I'll bounce through the craters
and fly, float and jump."

"I'll gaze at the blackness, be close to the stars,
and planets like Mercury, Venus and Mars."

"But really the thing
that I most want to see
is the beautiful Earth
staring back up at me."

Tessa dreams her big dream just like all children do
but she's really not sure how to make it come true.

"Now why the long face dear?" her Grandma inquires.
"You can go to the moon if that's what you desire."

"But Grandma, I'm stupid, I don't know enough,
and finding a rocket is going to be tough."

"How dare you be like this,

you'll get there one day,"

START WORKING AND TRYING,

YOU WILL FIND A WAY!

"Ok then, I'll do it! I'll fly by myself,"
she shouts and then grabs at more books from the shelf.

"I'll build a big space-ship that's three stories high"...

...but sadly for Tessa these boxes don't fly.

"Oh Tessa you fruitcake,
you do make me smile,
a rocket of boxes?
That might take a while."

"A rocket of boxes
to go to the moon?
What will you try next,
a giant hot-air balloon?"

But Tessa won't hear this,

"I don't like this talk"

"Just watch me,

I'll get there,"

I'M GOING TO WALK!

She storms
out the cottage
and into the gloom,
her path through
the grayness
lit-up
by the moon.

She marches through forest,
through snow and through ice,
whilst viewing in wonder
the best Northern Lights.

She's walking for miles,
through night and through day.
"There must be some people
who'll show me the way."

She wanders through valleys
where wide rivers flow...

...to deserts with cacti and real Navajo!

"My Tessa, you're here!" the Chief cheerfully said,
whilst shaking the feathers she wore on her head.
"Why have you come walking? What do you require?"

"To get to the moon,
that is what I desire."

"Come here round the fire
where we like to commune,
to harness the power of the
mighty great moon."

They jump, twirl and clap
shedding old fears and dread.
They dance for their dreams
for the year up ahead.

"Don't hold back now Tessa,
no time to be shy,
come dance with the moon
that is filling the sky!"

She springs on her toes,
throws her doubts
at the moon,
AND SHE CHOOSES FOR SURE
THAT SHE'LL MAKE IT THERE SOON.

She is back on her journey
and hikes through the night,
over Rockies and Andes,
the moon is her light.

To darkest Peru
where the jungle is found,
the Amazon stretching
for miles around.

She meets some Shipibo,
some real jungle folk,
they sit round and sing
whilst they puff on some smoke.

"So why are you here?"
the Shipibo inquire.

"To get to the moon,
that is what I desire".

"Come stand in the light
where we like to commune,
to harness the power
of the mighty great moon."

They sing "PACHAMAMA"
and throw their heads high,
"Mother Earth give our Tessa
the power to fly!"

The song gives a vision,
she's fighting a snake!
She can't let it hurt her,
moon mission's at stake.

Calling out to Shipibo
"What shall I do now?"

"You don't need to ask
you already know how!"

She kicks out and punches,
her hands held aloft.
She's so big and scary
the snake slithers off!

The vision has shown
what she needed to see,
THE GREAT STRENGTH AND POWER
IN THE SPACE-GIRL TO BE.

She's CHOSEN HER PLAN and she KNOWS THAT SHE'S STRONG,
but being a space-girl still feels a bit wrong.

A moon trip is tricky, she doesn't know how,
and on her big journey where will she go now?

So as sunset looms closer Tessa's happy to see
in the distance Indonesia, and it's island, Bali.

The feeling is calm as she stumbles to land,
the people are praying with their heads in their hands.

A girl dressed in white waddles round with a grin,
"It's time for Purnama, when we look deep within."

"Is that why you're here,
is that what you require?"

"To get to the moon,
that is what I desire."

"Come and stand by the shrine
and I'll show what we do
to harness the power
of the mighty great moon."

"We give gifts of flowers to become wise and whole,
be complete like the moon in our heart, mind and soul.
Like the glow of the moon on the dark of the night,
WE NEED DARK IN OURSELVES FOR OUR LIGHT TO SHINE BRIGHT."

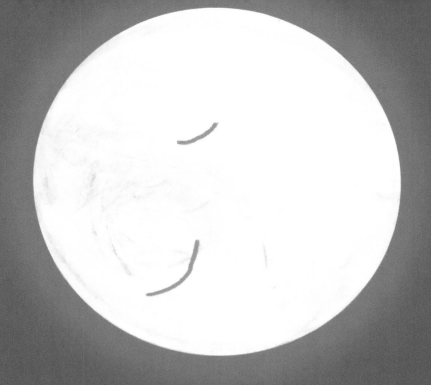

Leaning back, gazing up, in the dark she feels weightless,

in the light of the moon, TESSA FINDS HER OWN GREATNESS.

Tessa's walking back home with the moon up above,
WHILST HOLDING HER CHOICE AND HER POWER AND SELF-LOVE.

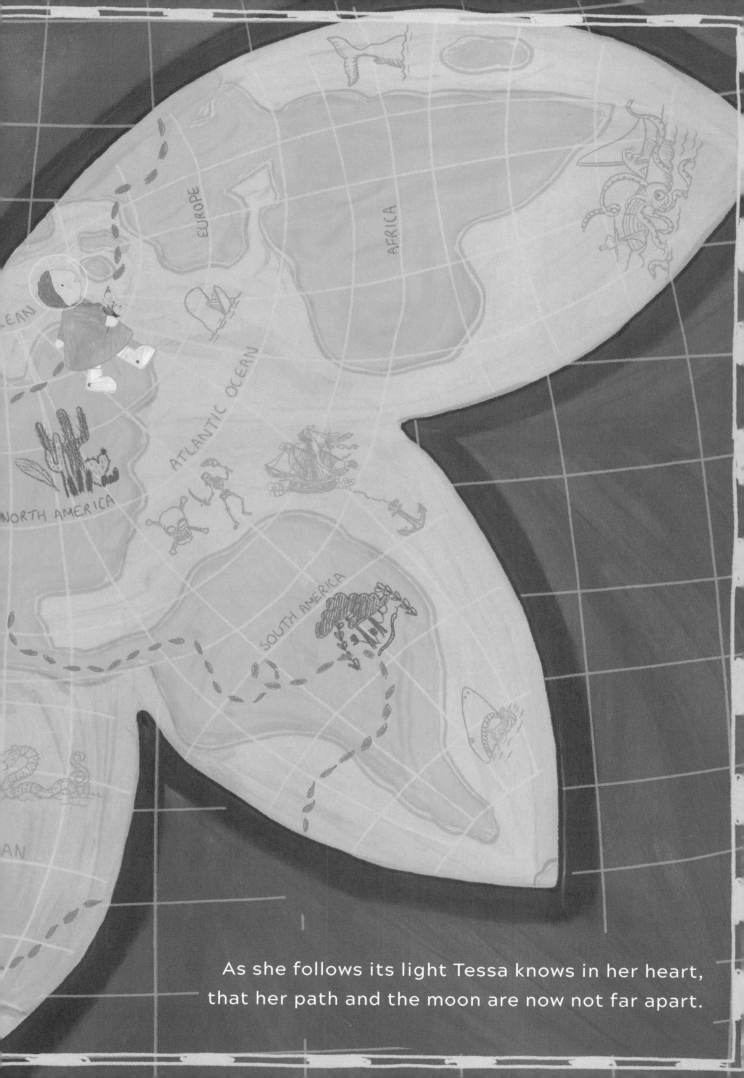

As she follows its light Tessa knows in her heart,
that her path and the moon are now not far apart.

She strides through the door, "Grandma guess where where I've been?"
Looking round at the room, Gran's nowhere to be seen.

In the quiet empty house Tessa's eyes start to tear,
"Why try walk to the moon when I could have stayed here?"

But she hears Grandma say, "What's that terrible noise?
Trying to walk to the moon was an excellent choice!"

"I'm so happy to know that you followed your dream,
I was there at the start, I am part of your team. "

"So don't worry about me, I have had my big day.
You keep working and trying, and YOU WILL FIND A WAY!"

So she stops all the noise and is starting to plot,
how she'll get to the moon one day, NO MATTER WHAT!

She works hard and studies
and she runs at a pace,
does advanced Maths and Physics
so she understands Space.

But applying for NASA,
she is dealt with a blow,

WE NEED SOMEONE MUCH SMARTER,
AND YOU'RE STILL FAR TOO SLOW.

But our Tessa keeps going,
"I will not listen to,
all these voices that tell me
what I can or can't do."

"I will only succeed,
I won't settle for less."

And the space girl keeps trying,

until one day...

...are delighted to te'

She rules the control room and leads her space team,
just as she had hoped in her childhood moon dream.

So, say "goodbye" to Tessa, who knows one day VERY soon,
that she'll be the first woman to land on the moon.

She trusts that she'll get there and she's even more glad
for the story she can tell of the adventure she's had.

And as she looks from the rocket on this magical day,
Tessa sees Gran, like always, is one small step away.

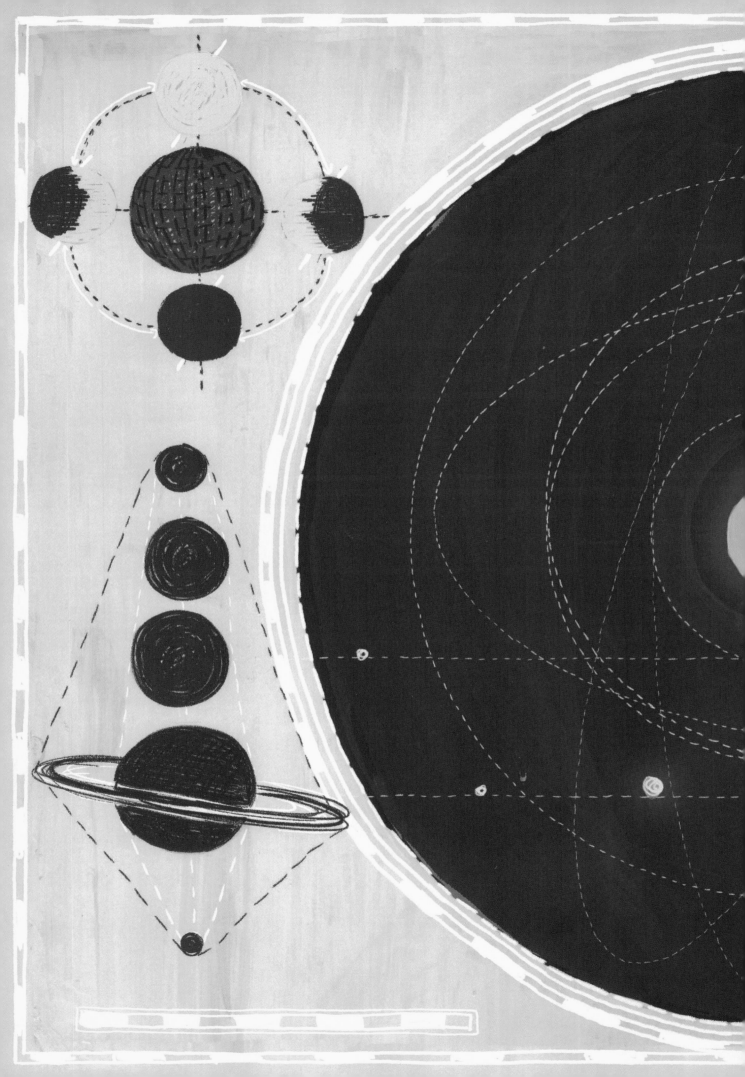

THIS BOOK IS DEDICATED TO THE FOLLOWING WONDERFUL PEOPLE
WHO SUPPORTED LITTLE TESSA ON KICKSTARTER
IN AN ASTRONOMICAL WAY:

JULIE YATES

CAROLINE AND FRED RICH

PETER GREENWOOD

SARAH AND OLLIE TALLON

BECKY STAPLES

NATASHA CZEGLEDY

DARRYL AND RUTH KNIGHTS

JACK AND ISLA BANBURY

JAKE, CHARLOTTE, FRIDA, HAMISH, EEYORE AND RASCAL

- THE CURTIS-CUSSINS FAMILY

THIS BOOK IS ALSO DEDICATED TO THE AMAZING LITTLE GIRL
WHO REMINDS ME EVERY DAY TO FOLLOW MY DREAMS,

ME.